SKELETON
FOR
DINNER

Margery Cuyler

Illustrated by
Will Terry

ALBERT WHITMAN & COMPANY
CHICAGO, ILLINOIS

For Sarah, with love—MC
For Betty—WT

Library of Congress Cataloging-in-Publication Data is on file with the publisher.

Text copyright © 2013 by Margery Cuyler
Illustrations copyright © 2013 by Will Terry
Published in 2013 by Albert Whitman & Company.
ISBN 978-0-8075-7398-3

Printed in China.
10 9 8 7 6 5 4 3 2 1 HH 18 17 16 15 14 13

For more information about Albert Whitman and Company,
please visit www.albertwhitman.com.

One day, Big Witch and Little Witch decided to brew a stew.

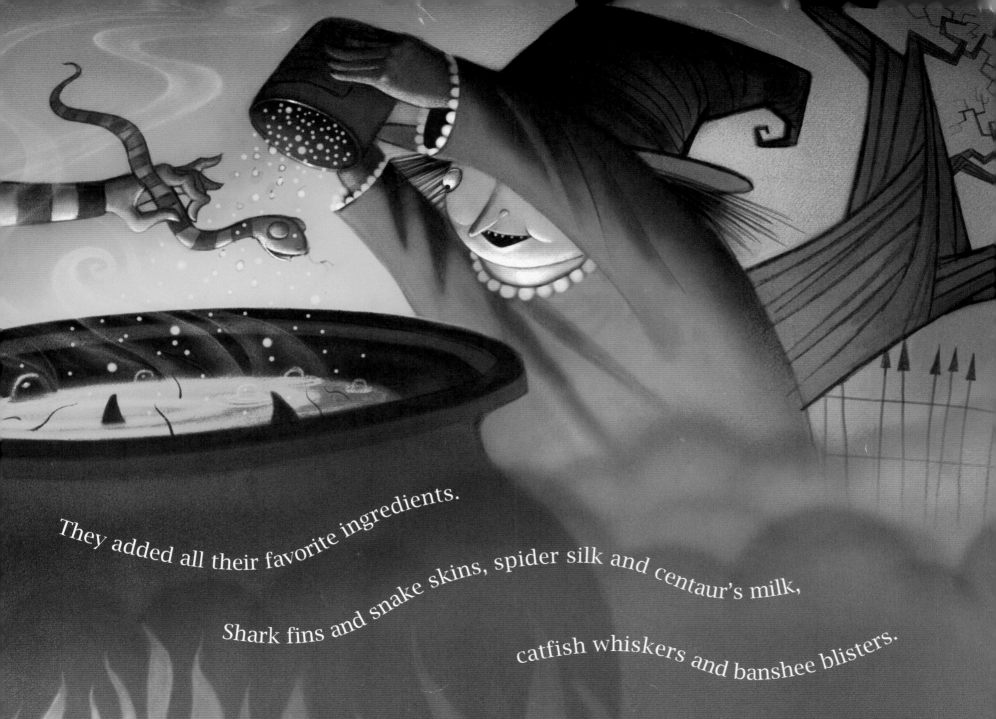

They added all their favorite ingredients.

Shark fins and snake skins, spider silk and centaur's milk,

catfish whiskers and banshee blisters.

Big Witch took a taste. "This is sooooo yummy," she said.
"Let's invite our friends for dinner."

"What fun!" said Little Witch. "I'll make a list.

Ghost,

Ghoul,

and..."

"Skeleton!" boomed Big Witch.

"We *must* have Skeleton for dinner."

Just then, Skeleton was clickity-clacking up the hill.

As he reached the top, he saw Little Witch's list pegged to a tree. He heard what Big Witch said to Little Witch.

"I think they want to have me for dinner!" cried Skeleton. "I don't want to be eaten!" His bones began to quake and shake.

For Dinner
1: Ghost
2. Ghoul
3. Skeleton

Before the witches saw him, he rat-a-bat-tatted down the hill...

and jingle-jangled as fast as he could to Ghost's.

"The witches want me in their stew,
and they want to eat you too," he screeched.

"Ohhhhh nooooo!" wailed Ghost,

and she floated after Skeleton.

They scooted by the graveyard where Ghoul was shoveling dirt.

"Where are you going in such a hurry?" he asked.

"The witches want us in their stew, and they want to eat you too," said Skeleton.

"Yikes," shouted Ghoul, "let's go hide."
And he dashed after the others.

Back on the hill, Little Witch said, "I'm off to invite our friends for dinner." And away she flew on her broomstick.

But when she got to Skeleton's, he was nowhere to be seen.

"Maybe he's at Ghost's," thought Little Witch.

But she didn't see anyone at Ghost's house either.

"I bet they're all at Ghoul's," thought Little Witch.

She zoomed to the graveyard. It was as quiet as the moon.

"Where is everybody?" said Little Witch. "How can I invite our friends for dinner if they've all disappeared?"

She flew back to the top of the hill. "I couldn't find anybody at home," she told Big Witch. "I guess we'll have to eat our stew all by ourselves. And I was really looking forward to our party."

She took down the sign and began to cry.

Crow flew down and picked it up. "I think I know what's wrong," he cawed and off he flew flapping his wings.

He went to Skeleton's. No Skeleton.

He went to Ghost's. No Ghost.

He went to Ghoul's. No Ghoul.

And then he saw footprints leading into the woods…

He followed them to a big tree.

Up, up, up he flew.

"What are *you* doing here?" asked Skeleton.

"I came to tell you that the witches want you to come for dinner."

"You mean they want to *eat* us for dinner," said Skeleton.

"No, they want to have you for dinner," said Crow.
"That means *invite* you for dinner."

"Ohhhhh," said Skeleton. "Well, that's different from what I thought.
I'm hungry. Let's go!"

So Skeleton, Ghost, and Ghoul came down from the tree.

They picked some poison ivy to take to the witches for their stew.

When they got to the top of the hill, the witches were so happy to see them, their faces lit up like jack-o'-lanterns.

"Come and eat!" shouted Big Witch.

"Have a seat!" shouted Little Witch.

"And we'll give you a treat," said both witches together.

"It looks so yummy," said Skeleton, "that I wish I had a tummy!"

And they all had fun eating the witches' stew together.